ONE'S LIFE

Charles Knevitt is a journalist, author and broadcaster and was the first Director of Inner City Aid, the Prince's charity launched in 1986 to encourage and support community development projects in deprived urban areas of the United Kingdom.

Born in America in 1952, of British parents, he was educated at Stonyhurst and the University of Manchester, School of Architecture. He was Architecture Correspondent of the *Sunday Telegraph* for four years before joining *The Times* in 1984, and was writer and presenter of Granada Television's award-winning documentary 'Rebuilding the Region' in its New North series in 1987.

He is the author or editor of seven books including *Space on Earth*, a companion to the six-part Anglia Television series for Channel Four on which he was consultant; *Monstrous Carbuncles*; and, with Nick Wates, *Community Architecture*. He collects cartoons as a hobby.

'The Very Important Person'

ONE'S LIFE

— A —
CARTOON BIOGRAPHY
OF HRH THE
PRINCE OF WALES
—

CHARLES KNEVITT

FOREWORD BY
SPIKE MILLIGAN

MICHAEL JOSEPH
LONDON

For Special K

The author would like to thank the following for their contributions to *One's Life*:
Anne Cowlin, my secretary, for her masterful management of the project;
Deborah Pownall, picture researcher; David Gwyn Jones for the inspired title;
Sara Drake, my agent (now moved on) for clinching the contract; Vivien James,
Sally Holloway and Patricia Walters, of Michael Joseph; Spike Milligan for his
Foreword; Canon Sebastian Charles and Elizabeth Zub, of Inner City Aid; Mike
Gowen and Sue Walker, of sponsors Faber-Castell; and by no means least, all the
cartoonists who so generously agreed to releasing their copyright material,
especially Trog, Marc and Mac; and the newspapers and magazines who
promptly dealt with requests for prints, especially the *Sun*.

One's Life is sponsored by A. W. Faber-Castell (UK) Ltd, Crompton Road,
Stevenage, Herts SG1 2EF, England. A Polymath Publication for Inner City Aid.

Faber-Castell

MICHAEL JOSEPH LTD

Published by the Penguin Group
27 Wrights Lane, London W8 5TZ, England
Viking Penguin Inc., 40 West 23 Street, New York, New York 10010, USA
Penguin Books Australia Ltd, Ringwood, Victoria, Australia
Penguin Books Canada Ltd, 2801 John Street, Markham, Ontario, Canada L3R 1B4
Penguin Books (NZ) Ltd, 182–190 Wairau Road, Auckland 10, New Zealand

Penguin Books Ltd, Registered Offices, Harmondsworth, Middlesex, England.

First published 1988

Selection and text copyright © Charles Knevitt, 1988

Foreword copyright © Spike Milligan Productions, 1988
For cartoon copyrights, see page 160

0 7181 3177 0
A CIP catalogue record for this book is
available from the British Library

Typeset in Caledonia by Goodfellow & Egan, Cambridge
Printed and bound in Great Britain by Butler and Tanner Ltd,
Frome, Somerset

Contents

Foreword

My God! Does the man know it? November the 14th 1988 (year of our Lord and Tesco's) the well known Prince of Charles Wales and district will be forty in old currency – in decimal counting he'll be 83p. Stop the calendar, let the Prince off at the Regain Hair Centre for balding Windsors. I tell you if we let the Prince of Charles go past 40, Superintendant Anderton/God will have him for speeding on the Queen's highway and have his royal leg clamped. No, we must stop Prince of Charles going past forty – I mean if that went on he would become the Prince of Barbara Cartland with his/her face covered in flour snow and lipstick, I mean can you see that fatal Nov 14th morning at Highgrove — ?

The Royal-Boiled-Eggs-For-Breakfast-Room. At gunpoint Lady Di is forcing the Royal chicken to lay an egg for Prince Henry. 'Lightly boiled or else' she says. Meanwhile a liveried childminder is trying to wrestle an axe from Prince William. There comes a fanfare composed on a betting slip by the late Ronnie Scott, who has just discovered his mother was a man. A man-flap in the back door opens and in comes a draught followed by the Prince of Charles dressed as the Duchy of Cornwall in a Lord Snowdon motorised wheelchair; he ducks as an axe goes past his head. 'Curses', says little Prince William, 'I was nearly the heir to the throne.' The Prince of Charles kisses Lady Di and the childminder. 'This could mean promotion for you,' he says to the latter (I forgot to say there was a latter in the room). 'Darling', he says. 'Do you mean me?' says the childminder. 'The Tower for you,' says enraged Prince of Charles. 'I'd prefer the basement flat', says childminder. Quickly the Prince agrees a rent and a small advance, three paces. 'Now dear' he addressed Lady Di 'Stupendous news today, I'm forty.' So, that day he was Charles Forte. Tomorrow he would be the Prince of Charles again. 'What did you say?' said Lady Di catching the chicken's egg as it shot out. 'I said,' said I, Prince of Charles, 'I'm forty,' Lady Di reeled back, reeled forwards and finally reeled upright. 'Take him away,' she said, 'and bring me a fresh Prince!'

Well I have known this Prince since I met him at his Auntie Margaret's home – where we had dinner with his Mum, Dad and sister. He was a lad of fourteen and I wasn't. First thing that struck me was his sense of humour – that has, whenever I meet him, been ongoing. My God, how he likes to laugh, he himself being no slouch when it comes to telling a funny story. Like his father, he speaks out not just for himself but those *millions*, who, on the face of giant businesses and bureaucracies, feel helpless. This book of cartoons is to be sold to benefit his own charity, Inner City Aid. Bear in mind that, if these cartoons had been done about Henry VIII, their creators' heads would all be stuck on pikes outside St James's Palace – we've come a long way since then. God bless the Prince of Wales, but don't forget the rest of us.

Spike

SPIKE MILLIGAN

Royal road to the future

One's Life, The First Forty Years

Cartoonists have always been among the most perceptive social commentators of their day, as well as persuasive campaigners for a better world. With a few strokes of the pen and still fewer well-chosen words they can convey what it might take a leader writer a score of carefully composed paragraphs to get across with infinitely less precision and wit. And, after politicians, it is members of the Royal Family to whom the cartoonists turn most frequently for their inspiration, for there is always a receptive audience for the doings and sayings of those who reign – though no longer rule – over us.

Prince Charles is the twenty-first English Prince of Wales and, like many of his predecessors, is frequently lampooned by contemporary cartoonists. But he can be thankful that the monarchy today is in far better odour with the public than in previous centuries: James Gillray's merciless caricatures of the debauched thirty-year-old Prince who later became King George IV, and Max Beerbohm's

depiction of a dunce-like Prince Albert Edward, later King Edward VII, serve as painful reminders to the present Royal Family that their ancestors were not always illustrious or treated with due deference.

As Prince Charles remarked in 1978: 'I cannot help but reflect on how politely we have been treated, compared to the way in which King George III and his family, for instance, were treated by the eighteenth and nineteenth-century cartoonists, such as Rowlandson. However, even if the cartoonists have shown, here and there, a dash of irreverence or a bit of satire, they obviously do not mean it *too* seriously.'

Sympathy – nay, reverence – for King George VI and then Queen Elizabeth II when they came to the throne killed off the art of caricaturing monarchy for a while. An exception was the work of cartoonist David Low. Buckingham Palace warned during the war that royalty was not a suitable subject matter for cartoons, but Low took the opportunity of the Queen's Coronation in 1953 to hit back in the *Manchester Guardian*. It was, of course, the first televised crowning of a monarch and his 'Morning After' showed a grim-faced Queen staring out of a television set as John Citizen recovered from the previous day's expensive celebrations. The cartoon also broke with the post-war convention of not showing a royal face. There was a predictable outcry from readers: within days, the editor had received no fewer than 575 letters.

A decade later, Trog went much further, in the *Spectator*, when he parodied Lord Snowdon's recent appointment as a photographer for the *Sunday Times* in a less than flattering light. Gerald Scarfe's cruel distortions in *Private Eye* – as

*Cartoonists have no qualms about caricaturing the Prince's
larger than average ears.*

wickedly savage in their execution as anything which appeared during the reigns of
Georges I, II and III – opened the floodgates. But very often the reaction from
those targeted (or their relatives) proved to be just the opposite of what you might
expect. When Jensen, in the *Sunday Telegraph*, had the ghost of Queen Elizabeth
I visiting the present much-travelled Queen, saying, 'My more spirited subjects
used to globetrot while *I* stayed at home. What are all *your* Sir Walter Raleighs
doing?', there were complaints that our monarch was depicted as frumpish and
middle-aged. But Prince Philip still bought the original!

Prince Charles is an avid collector of cartoons, many depicting himself, which
he keeps in the visitors' loos at Kensington Palace. On one occasion I tried to
purchase the original of a cartoon, published that morning, of the Prince talking to
his plants (back cover), only to be told: 'Sorry, Diana has just beaten you to it!'

With the growth of mass-circulation newspapers and magazines this century,
cartoon audiences are far greater than ever they were in the age of Gillray. And
with the tabloids' obsession with members of the Royal Family there is a new edge
– some would say, viciousness – to some of the cartoons themselves. As Bernard
Levin wrote in 1976: 'Cartoonists and caricaturists are the great columnists of our
day.'

Cartoonists felt the need, not so long ago, to 'put their top hats on' when
portraying royalty, out of respect. Nowadays, they have lost that over-deference
and have no qualms about caricaturing the Prince's larger than average ears or
showing him in all manner of situations and poses, including convict, guru and

wimp. Imagine that great cartoonist H.M. Bateman, if he were alive today, illustrating Prince Charles as 'The Man Who . . . Talked to His Plants . . . Tilted at Carbuncles . . . Told Lumberjacks to Search for the Inner Man'!

While the attitudes of the newspapers and cartoonists have changed dramatically in the lifetime of the Prince, so too has the Royal Family. The Sixties were the watershed. John Osborne described the Royal Family as 'the gold filling in the mouth of decay'; Princess Margaret's marriage to society photographer (and commoner) Antony Armstrong-Jones caused considerable comment; the indiscretions of 'Crawfie', Marion Crawford, the Queen's ex-governess in her memoirs, provided the source of much titillation and gossip. While the occasional royal wedding was always a time for national rejoicing and celebration, it gradually dawned on the Palace that positive steps needed to be taken to secure a non-republican future. Although King Farouk of Egypt had predicted, in 1951, that by the year 2000 the only kings left would be the Kings of England and those in a pack of playing cards, the future of the family 'firm', as King George VI dubbed it, was believed to be at stake. Television was chosen as the medium to convey the new image.

King George V had instituted the monarch's annual broadcast to the nation on the wireless in 1932. In 1957 it transferred to television and was relayed to the Commonwealth but was cancelled by the present Queen in 1969. It was replaced, to some extent, by a series of more intimate portraits of the Royal Family: an interview with Prince Philip on BBC Television's *Panorama*; an interview with the Prince of Wales, in which he discussed what sort of girl he might marry; and a complete documentary called *The Royal Family*. Prince Charles may have stated, on one occasion, that 'The monarchy is one of the oldest professions in the world', but, as Prince Philip also remarked, in a television interview in 1968: 'The monarchy is part of the fabric of the country. And, as the fabric alters, so the monarchy and its people's relations to it alter.'

As late as 1848, Queen Victoria was still proclaiming the divine right of monarchy, but by the 1960s the Sovereign and her family had acquired a common touch. They were more accessible to Joe Public and seemed to have a role as relevant to the future as to the past. It was in this atmosphere that Prince Charles grew up and started to face the modern Press – with its anarchic breed of latterday Gillrays.

'Humour,' wrote Malcolm Muggeridge, one of the first critics of the Royal Family, in 1957, 'is practically the only thing about which the English are utterly serious.' And almost from the moment he was born, on 14 November 1948, Prince Charles began to be taken humorously as well as seriously.

As the first son (and heir apparent) he was at once Duke of Cornwall, in the English peerage, and Duke of Rothesay, Earl of Carrick and Baron of Renfrew, in the Scottish peerage. He was also Lord of the Isles and Prince and Great Steward – or Seneschal – of Scotland. His titles Prince of Wales and Earl of Chester were not conferred until 1958. But at various times he has also been known as HRH and The

Boss (to his staff), Chuck and Wales (to his friends), Taffy Windsor or Wales (in the Navy) and Brian or Heir of Sorrows (to readers of *Private Eye*). Auberon Waugh calls him Bat Ears (following in the tradition of King George VI, who was known as Bat Lugs at Dartmouth). He has on various occasions been called many other things – from Fishface (by his wife) to Pompous and Pommy Bastard, while in Australia – but we will not dwell on those here. The name he simply hates being called is 'Prince': 'It makes me sound like a police dog.'

Although subsequently burdened by these titles and nicknames, Prince Charles was christened Charles Philip Arthur George Mountbatten-Windsor, inheriting his surname from both his mother and his father. However, the Queen later reverted her name, and that of Prince Charles and Princess Anne, by royal decree, to her family name of Windsor. On the Prince and Princess's name-switch Prince Philip (the Mountbatten) remarked, 'It makes them sound like bastards' and himself just 'a bloody amoeba'.

In good time, of course, Prince Charles will become King Charles III, at which stage he will be the first king to follow five successive generations of unbroken descent down the royal family tree since the Plantagenets seven hundred years ago.

In the ever-quoted soliloquy from *As You Like It*, William Shakespeare suggests a man plays seven parts upon the world's stage – 'His acts being seven ages' – from birth to death. Prince Charles has already played at least five, from shy schoolboy to 'Action Man' in the services, Romeo, husband and father, and today, philosopher to some, rebel to others, Renaissance Man to a few, and saint (and potential martyr?) to at least one royal observer. The complexities of the man who would be king, now he has reached his second coming of age, have no doubt contributed to the present state of media analysis and confusion as to his actual role – a confusion which he seems to share.

'It is sad to say, but I have no real job except that of being Prince of Wales,' said the future King Edward VIII at the age of twenty-one. He had the job for twenty-five years. Likewise, Prince Charles seems racked by anxiety that he is not doing enough, or not doing what he does in the right way, and sometimes threatens to quit speaking out on important public issues, even though all the evidence, in frequent opinion polls, shows that he carries the weight of Great British public opinion on his side. Let's all hope that he fulfils the American statesman Benjamin Franklin's prediction that 'at twenty years of age the will reigns; at thirty the wit; and at forty the judgement'; and that the Prince decides it's worth staying the course. His early mentor, Lord Mountbatten, told him, after all: 'In this business you can't afford to be a shrinking violet.'

'Happy Birthday, Your Highness – key-of-the-door-day I
believe'

As matters stand it will most likely be well into the twenty-first century before the Prince becomes King. The Queen, who has already reigned for thirty-five years, could conceivably exceed Queen Victoria's record of sixty-three years and seven months. King Edward VIII's abdication, after less than a year, set a precedent which none – least of all the present Queen – wishes to follow. King William IV was almost sixty-five before he was crowned. As the Prince himself remarked in a speech, in 1974: 'Queen Victoria in her eighties was more known, more revered and a more important part of the life of the country than she had ever been. Retirement, for a monarch, is not a good idea.'

The Prince has had to come to terms with a long wait, while still remaining very much in the public eye. One of his most effective weapons in dealing with the trappings of fame – not least media attention – is an ability to laugh at himself: 'If only more politicians were capable of laughing at themselves occasionally, the world would be a happier and more sensible place,' he told the then editor of *Punch*, William Davis. 'As far as I am concerned a sense of humour is what keeps me sane and I would probably have been committed to an institution long ago were it not for the ability to see the funny side of life.'

He also believes in being who he is rather than living up to other people's expectations or wishes of him: 'I was asked whether I concentrated on developing my 'image' – as if I were some kind of washing powder, presumably with a special blue whitener. I have absolutely no idea what my image is and therefore I intend to go on being myself to the best of my ability.'

By nature the Prince is a very private individual behind the public myth, and has described himself as 'a romantic'. Unlike his father, he is neither competitive nor aggressive, but shares Prince Philip's conservatism, tempered with more obvious social concern. With undoubted charm and charisma, he is also tenacious and occasionally stubborn, sensitive, thoughtful, perceptive, with a sharp self-deprecating wit. No wonder his future wife described him, after their first meeting, as 'pretty amazing'.

A countryman at heart – 'I can't stand cities' – he once professed: 'If I wasn't who I am, I would love to have been a farmer.' But he also loves danger: after he calmly managed to disentangle himself from his rigging (with only eight hundred feet between him and oblivion) on his first ever parachute jump, he commented on it simply as 'a rather hairy experience'.

But more recently, as the most outspoken member of the Royal Family, and with many 'alternative' interests, some people have interpreted the man as something of an oddball. The first to suggest this, when the Prince was still in his twenties, was the gossip columnist Lady Olga Maitland: 'Mark my words, there's something wrong with that boy.' His missionary zeal in pursuing his various causes has also led to him being dubbed 'the spiritual wing of the Royal Family, the Mother Theresa of Buckingham Palace'. The tabloid Press, in the habit of building icons (with him, at the time of his wedding) only to knock them down again, now often likes to portray him as either an eccentric or a complete wet.

Because he is driven by his heart rather than by his head in much of what he says, he is frequently misunderstood. 'As far as I can make out, I'm about to become a Buddhist monk or live halfway up a mountain, or only eat grass. I'm not quite as bad as that,' he protested to the *Sunday Times* in 1985. Nor can there be any doubt that many would like to silence his criticisms of the status quo and are jealous of his ability to motivate social idealism and generate widespread public acclaim.

The Press's excesses have twice caused the Queen to summon Fleet Street editors for a dressing down, first after the *Sunday Mirror* reported a meeting between the Prince and Lady Diana on board 'the Royal love train' in a Wiltshire railway siding (an incident which was denied by the Palace); and three years later

*Mark my words, there's something
wrong with that boy.*

*I was asked whether I
concentrated on developing my
image – as if I were some kind of
washing powder, presumably with
a special blue whitener.*

*George Bernard Shaw maintained
that 'every man over forty is a
scoundrel'.*

when the Press were causing an unwelcome intrusion at Sandringham. Not surprisingly, many of these displays of journalistic over-enthusiasm were leapt upon by the cartoonists of the daily papers. True, it is in the nature of cartoons to make people feel uncomfortable as well as laugh, but the implicit understatement of the genre as it has been practised in Britain for decades seems, at last, to be succumbing to the American tendency to exaggerate. No doubt this results in a huge response from outraged readers in the form of the letters which editors so crave, but the knighthoods once bestowed on the likes of Low and Bernard Partridge seem less frequent of late, perhaps for the same reason.

One wonders how W. B. Pitkin, the man who coined the saying 'Life begins at forty' more than half a century ago, would consider the cartoonists' view of the Prince of Wales now he has reached this numerical watershed? More favourably, perhaps, than George Bernard Shaw who maintained that 'every man over forty is a scoundrel'. The Prince in fact has several cartoon personae, depending on who is drawing him. None has yet devised the definitive view, as Vicky did of 'Supermac' or Low with his TUC carthorse and 'Colonel Blimp', but certainly Marc's portrait (front cover) and Trog's gun-slinging Prince facing Mrs. Thatcher over who decides the fate of the inner cities (page 93) come close.

In this television age perhaps our perception of celebrities is governed as much by *Spitting Image* puppets and voiceovers as the more genteel satire of cartoons. Yet through their successful distillation of social history into just a few marks on paper and an apposite punchline, cartoons are sure to remain among the most potent influences on our view of the world.

'Cartoonists, almost more than anyone else, help to relieve unnecessary tension, deflate ridiculous pomposity and emphasise the funny side of something that may threaten to become dangerously serious,' wrote the Prince in 1978. 'It is also considerably easier to libel someone pictorially (and get away with it) than it is to do so by the printed word!'

Forty years of 'one's life' have provided us with much mirth over the breakfast table. *One's Life*, both a record and a celebration, offers a second chance to enjoy the cartoonists' interpretation of what was – and an opportunity to speculate on what is still to come.

'Look, Mummy – the stork's come back!'

Born to be King

Life for Charles Philip Arthur George Mountbatten-Windsor began at 9.14 p.m. on the chilly night of 14 November 1948. Princess Elizabeth gave birth to the 7lb 6oz baby boy, thirty-ninth in descent from Alfred the Great, in the Bohl Room of Buckingham Palace. Queen Mary thought the baby bore a remarkable resemblance to Prince Albert. Five thousand people were outside in the Mall when the official communiqué was hung on the railings, and film star David Niven stood in the crowd, helping to persuade them to disperse so that the Princess could get a good night's sleep.

It was not long before the British fashion industry cottoned on to this royal asset, voting him the Best Dressed Man of 1954. He was five. For his eighth birthday an official portrait was commissioned by the society photographer Antony Armstrong-Jones, and shortly afterwards the young Prince was off to Hill House Prep School for two terms. Later he followed in his father's footsteps to Cheam School, where he won a medal for high-jumping, and then to Gordonstoun. Here, the Prince's initiation consisted of being ducked, fully-clothed, in a cold bath. He sometimes thought about running away, but his grandmother, Queen Elizabeth the Queen Mother, persuaded him not to and instead to face up to his spartan schooling. History, geography and painting were his favourite subjects, but, like his mother, he loathed mathematics. In 1963 Prince Charles made headlines around the world when, at the age of fourteen, he ordered a glass of cherry brandy at a pub in Stornoway during a school outing. 'Hardly had I taken a sip than the whole world exploded around my ears,' the Prince said. 'Well, I thought it was the end of the earth. I was all ready to pack my bags and leave for Siberia . . .'

After Gordonstoun, he spent two terms at Timbertop, in Australia, where the emphasis on physical fitness and self-reliance in the curriculum at his previous school stood him in very good stead. His university education followed at Cambridge, where he developed his love of music, acting, polo and flying, and later at Aberystwyth, where he learnt Welsh before his investiture as Prince of Wales in 1969.

The morning of the great event he kept seeing an interview with himself that he had pre-recorded for television. 'It's always me,' he complained. 'I'm getting rather sick of my face!' Later, he said of the investiture 'I do enjoy ceremonies.' The day's design and media impressario was Lord Snowdon, who wore a tunic of dark hunting green and a belt of black corded silk, an outfit which, according to the Duke of Norfolk, made him look like 'a bell-hop at a hotel'. Prince Charles, by contrast, received nothing but praise from the Mayor of Caernarvon, who said: 'You could have put a suit of armour on that lad and sent him off to Agincourt!'

'I circled twice for the benefit of
the crowd before making a perfect
two-point landing'

'What's the matter with 'em these days? Mine's been so excited
about something, she stuck three nappy pins in me over the
weekend'

'You and your "Let's call at the Palace and invite him to our
New Year party while his mum and dad are away".'

Happy . . . returns

'Look what I got from a boy at school'

'I've called to see if the boxing gloves we supplied for Prince Charles's birthday were satisfactory'

'He *only* had one cherry brandy. You're *tight as a drum and
driving under the influence*'

'Can ye no play "Charlie is ma darlin" – as a lament?'

'He's just heard there's a vacancy'

'Careful, it might be His Royal 'Ighness!'

Caernarvon prepares for the Investiture

'Mine doesn't help me much with my English'

'We're leaving no stone unturned, Your Grace'

'No, it wasn't Welsh nationalists, Your Highness, it was
souvenir hunters!'

'*Ask His Royal Highness to come to my office when he's finished
his solo flight*'

'*I suppose we did send them to the right schools?*'

Huntin', Shootin' and Fishin' *et al*

Prince Charles, though he enjoys some of his ancestors' pastimes, tends to pursue more macho hobbies including some which, on three separate occasions, have almost proved fatal: when parachuting in 1971, playing polo in 1980 and skiing in 1988. But then he has said: 'I believe in living life dangerously and I think a lot of others do too.' Living dangerously 'helps you appreciate life.'

As regards music, learning the piano at prep school proved unfruitful, so he graduated to the trumpet (at which he was also poor) then the cello, which he played in the university orchestra at Cambridge. He was also good on the banjo (the Duke of Windsor often strummed the 'Red Flag' on the banjo when he was at university). Prince Charles enjoyed listening to The Seekers, The Beatles and jazz, but more especially Bach, Beethoven and Mozart. Berlioz sometimes reduces him to tears. As for the only song he knows by heart – the Prince says it is the Goons' 'Ying-Tong Song'.

Like his younger brother, Edward, the Prince showed early promise as an actor. He likes mimicking people and at Gordonstoun he played the Scottish King in *Macbeth* and the Pirate King in the *Pirates of Penzance*. At Cambridge he took part in revue sketches, including one prompted by the dustman who used to wake him up by singing under his college window. 'To my regret, when I leave Cambridge the opportunities for acting, for crouching in uncollected dustbins and receiving custard pies in an ecclesiastical face, will be limited,' he said at the time.

He fishes, has raced horses (with varying success) and loves hunting. Shooting has sometimes led him into controversy: in 1975 he was accused of being 'hooked on killing animals for kicks' by the League Against Cruel Sports; and in 1978 he was dubbed Hooligan of the Year by the Royal Society for the Prevention of Cruelty to Animals. 'Not content with fox hunting,' said Mr John Bryant, the Prince 'killed five wild pigs, pheasants and hare' while on a trip to Vienna. Even his old chum Spike Milligan was incensed, saying that the Royal Family were 'hunting junkies'. But the Prince's overriding passion remains polo, a sport at which his father also excelled. Once he was given a mount called Christine Keeler. 'I love the game, I love the ponies, I love the exercise,' he said. 'It's the one team game I can play.'

As for more sedentary activities, the Prince paints – his first ever school report recorded: 'Art: good and simply loves drawing and painting' – another talent he shares with his father. 'It's very rewarding, very hard work. And makes marvellous Christmas presents,' he said. He exhibited at the Royal Academy Summer Exhibition in 1987 under the name of Arthur George Carrick.

'Not only all fresh today, madam, but
all caught by Prince Charles'

'Charles!'

'Some day, my son, all this will be yours . . .'

'We hear they weren't amused!'

'OK, let's try it this way'

'We heard you were jumping again, Your Highness!'

'It takes quite a time to get the knack,' remarked the Prince
casually, following the announcement that Cowdray Polo Club
wishes to encourage teenagers to play polo

'*Let's hope he doesn't fall out of that!*'

'*Don't remove your crash helmet yet, Sir*'

'Could I have a word with you Simpson?'

'I'd stick to landscape painting if I were you, Your Highness!'

'No, no, those are William's – my sketches are over here'

'*Think yourself lucky we're blaming the horse!*'

'*It's just a question of getting them involved in more exciting things,*' *says Prince Charles discussing football hooligans*

Action Man and Eligible Bachelor

For obvious reasons, the Prince had been dubbed 'the world's most eligible bachelor' by the Press, and for several years, until his eventual marriage in 1981, he played a cat-and-mouse game which occupied much of their time. As he pursued his career in the Royal Navy and Royal Air Force, took part in a variety of active (and photogenic) sports, and acquired a £6,000 Aston Martin DB6 Volante, his other nickname, Action Man, became common parlance.

For a decade he entertained a bevy of beauties: Georgiana Russell, daughter of the British Ambassador to Madrid; Lady Jane Wellesley, daughter of the Duke of Wellington; Lucia Santa Cruz, daughter of the former Chilean Ambassador to the Court of St James's; Laura-Jo Watkins, from San Diego, whom he invited to watch his maiden speech in the House of Lords; Davina Sheffield, whose past was questioned by the Press; Princess Elizabeth of Yugoslavia, former fiancée of Richard Burton; Princess Caroline of Monaco; Princess Marie-Astrid of Luxembourg; and Lady Sarah Spencer, elder sister of Lady Diana.

He took tea with Barbra Streisand in Hollywood; dined with Farrah Fawcett-Majors at the Beverly Hilton then later at the Dorchester in London; and met Fiona Watson, twenty-three-year-old god-daughter of Lord Brownlow, whose job was 'to entertain him during his off-duty hours' when he began a short refresher course at RAF Cranwell. It soon came to light that Ms Watson had posed nude in *Penthouse* magazine three years earlier.

Matters got serious on several occasions. When Lady Leonora became engaged to the Fifth Earl of Lichfield in the mid-1970s, the Queen Mother remarked: 'What a pity. We were saving her for Charles.' Anna Wallace came close to being proposed to until she embarrassed the Prince at the Queen Mother's eightieth birthday party. The Prince once asked his grandmother to instruct Lady Jane on royal protocol and the role of his future wife before she decided she did not want to live in the permanent public gaze.

'Poor Jane Wellesley,' the Prince remarked about the Press's hounding of the girl. Of Princess Caroline he quipped: 'I have only met the girl once and they are trying to marry us off.' And of Princess Marie-Astrid: 'If I marry a Catholic, I'm dead. I've had it.' He managed to keep his sense of humour throughout, however. When, in 1979, he took twenty-four-year-old Sabrina Guinness, former nanny to Tatum O'Neal and Girl Friday to David Bowie, to the theatre, it was to see *Ain't Misbehavin'* at Her Majesty's!

The Prince survived several attempts to marry him off, the least discreet by President Nixon whose daughter Tricia, he remarked, was 'artificial and plastic'.

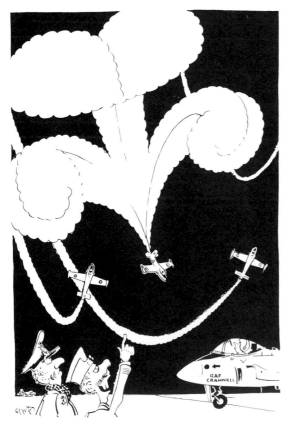

'That's the new boy, Sir.'

'I'll be at my Mum's for the week-end – you know
her address . . .'

'I told you he's barmy about hunting!'

'Why anyone should want to quit the Navy beats me'

'With the compliments of Eric Morley . . .'

'Not yet, Deirdre! Not yet!'

'Judging by your Bonnie Prince Charlie's waistline, food must be cheaper in Canada'

'He's never been the same since he met Jane!'

'Has Charlie mentioned anything about keeping you in the
manner to which you're accustomed?'

'I trust HRH Red Crow realises that last little ceremonial puff
made my daughter the future Queen of England'

'It's the end of the line, Ted – we can't keep supplying a royal
romance every time you have a crisis!'

'Thank heaven we've found how to keep the Sheilas at bay,
fellows!'

'Get that thing off! It's not Charles who's opening the
show!'

'*Even if you could marry him, you'd still be up against Anna
Wallace, Lady Jane Wellesley and the rest of 'em*'

'*An introductory offer, Your Highness. From the Enoch Powell
Marriage Bureau . . . friendships arranged, etc., etc.*'

Monarchs must be Protestants and may not marry Catholics. Continuing speculation
that the Prince was to marry Catholic Princess Marie-Astrid led the Ulster Unionist
MP Enoch Powell to speak out.

One's Trouble and Strife

'The Royal Family of England pulls off ceremonies the way the army of Israel pulls off commando raids,' said the *Boston Globe* on the occasion of Prince Charles's wedding. So it was that on 29 July 1981, at St. Paul's Cathedral, Prince Charles married Lady Diana Spencer, the 'girl next door' whom he had first met on a birthday visit to her parents' home at Althorp, Northamptonshire, in 1977. He had been twenty-nine, she had been sixteen. 'What a very amusing and jolly – and attractive – sixteen-year old she was,' said the Prince, who had been dating Diana's twenty-two-year-old elder sister, Lady Sarah, at the time.

He proposed to Diana three years later, over dinner *à deux* in his third-floor apartment at Buckingham Palace, just before she left for a holiday in Australia. He gave her a ring which cost a reputed £25,000, and suggested she think the matter over for a month before deciding if it was going to be 'too awful' living under intense public scrutiny for the rest of her life. The engagement was officially announced on 24 February 1981. Remarking on their twelve-year age difference, the Prince said: 'I just feel you are as old as you think you are', and 'Diana will certainly keep me young. I think I shall be exhausted.'

Lady Diana Spencer was born at Park House, Sandringham, and can count among her ancestors six American presidents, while her family tree shows such diverse relations as Oliver Cromwell, Sir Winston Churchill, Herman Goering, George Orwell, Gloria Vanderbilt, Lawrence of Arabia, the Aga Khan and the Marquis de Sade!

More than 2,300 people were invited to the wedding, a million people lined the streets to see the couple, and a further 750 million watched it on television throughout the world, the largest audience for any event on record. The bride wore a David and Elizabeth Emanuel crinoline in silk taffeta with huge, puffed sleeves, lace ruffles and bows. When she arrived at the altar, the Prince's first words were, 'You look wonderful', to which she replied, 'Wonderful for you.' During the ceremony the Princess nervously transposed her spouse's name, Charles Philip Arthur George to Philip Charles Arthur George. Afterwards, the Prince remarked, 'You married my father!' Later, in response to cries from the crowd in front of Buckingham Palace, they kissed publicly, setting a new precedent for royal weddings.

They went off on honeymoon to Gibraltar where they boarded the Royal Yacht *Britannia* for a Mediterranean cruise. The Prince had ordered a new piece of furniture on board – a double bed – and they set sail with a mere 311 other people. Their wedding gifts were estimated to be worth £10 million.

*'Her first words were "no comment".
She goes to the kindergarten where
Lady Diana Spencer works'*

Another romance?

Garland's spoof is based on the famous royal engagement
photograph, where the Prince appeared to be head and
shoulders taller than his fiancée. In fact he is one inch taller,
except when she's wearing high heels!

'Charles thinks His Grace's collar should be worn higher!'

Parting is such sweet sorrow

*'Surely even Willie Hamilton will admit that two can live as
cheaply as one!'*

*'I told her it's at St Paul's but she says they always have 'em
here'*

'We promise to put it back quick if it rains, officer!'

William Rushton's view of the royal wedding

'*It's all right, Sir, Basil the pigeon has been captured!*'

'**Di** isch mi ganzes Härz!' ('*Di is the love of my life!*')

'*Fasten your seat belt, Di, we're just passing over Spain!*'

'Away from it all . . . no photographers . . . no
reporters . . .'

'Hop it, you lot – he's a happily married man!'

'We should get some great shots from here!'

'I think it's a mistake to hold the fireworks display on GLC
territory!'

'You sure it wasn't someone
shopping for royal wedding
presents?'

'Playing up 'ell because she couldn't find her woolly egg
warmer on show'

'*Never mind the happy couple kissing in public – you two knock it off!*'

West-Enders

When in London, Prince Charles's family stays at Kensington Palace, known to insiders as KP or Kens Pal, and to the Press as Coronet Street, because several other members of the Royal family live there. But when the Prince first saw his new London home after his marriage, apartments eight and nine of KP, where King George I and King George II housed their mistresses, he described them as a 'pigeon loft'. Architects from the Department of the Environment spent six years and £900,000 doing the place up.

It was at KP that the famous encounter between Bob Geldof and young Prince William took place, which the rock star and fund-raiser relates in his autobiography *Is That It?* Wombat, or Wills, as the Prince and Princess's first-born son is known, accused the megastar of being dirty, with scruffy hair and wet shoes. Geldof told him: 'Your hair's scruffy, too', to which Wombat countered, before he left the room, 'No it's not, my mummy brushed it.'

Prince William was born on 21 June 1982 after a difficult pregnancy. He made history by being the first heir to the throne to be born in a hospital. Prince Charles attended the birth and soon learnt to change nappies.

Prince Henry, known as Harry, was born in 1984. The press were quick to note that his aunt and uncle, Princess Anne and Captain Mark Phillips, were missing from his christening. Months earlier, they had fixed a shooting party for the very same day and were loathe to give it up.

The children call their parents Mummy and Papa. Prince Charles calls his wife 'Diana, love', the Princess calls her husband 'Darling' or, on one occasion publicly, 'Fishface'! They often use false identities when they travel abroad: the Prince has called himself Charlie Chester, Mr Postle, Renfrew and Sir John Riddell (the name of his Private Secretary). When she went for wedding dress fittings, the Princess used the alias Deborah Smythson Wells. Together they sometimes travel under the names Chester, Hardy or Smith!

The Princess has carved out her own niche since her marriage. The former school hockey team captain who uses the call-sign 'Disco Di from KP' when phoning friends, was described by Prudence Glynn, fashion editor of *The Times*, as 'a fashion disaster in her own right' in 1981. Today she is the most glamorous and most photographed woman in the world.

The children sometimes prove a handful for their parents. At one point young Wills took to flushing his toys down the lavatory and throwing tantrums. He is even reported as once having dangled his younger brother from an upstairs window at Kensington Palace!

'It's arrived!'

'And I'm a bit worried about William lately!'

'Shush, you'll soon get used to it'

'Dad, I've hammered out the dent in your car!'

'Great news darling – I'm signed up to star with Noddy in
Noddy and Big Ears *at Buck House*'

'Yes, I'm terribly worried about the effect these shows
have on him – it's not any good for Wills either'

'OK, Your Highness, I won't call you Roger but let me at least
look after your robes'

'William is so thrilled, Ma'am – he came straight in and started
rearranging the nursery'

'Charles liked me, Diana liked me, William wasn't sure'

'This one has a portrait of Willie
Hamilton in it!'

'All this fuss! Honestly, Charles, who wants to walk around
year after year with the same hair style?'

'Oh look, Harry, I've found another
Easter egg to crack'

'William! Harry! – you're not supposed to open your presents
till Christmas!'

'Very brave of you, Your Highness, to let your sons take
charge'

'I've had to spank him again, he keeps slipping your blasted
opera tapes into my Walkman'

'I just hope you never meet Eddie Kidd!'

'Now you've got their autographs, perhaps we can go home'

'*You can switch Beethoven off right now, Charles*'

'Really, Charles – don't you think you're making rather a fuss
about nothing?'

'Don't glare at me . . . It was Fergie who sat on it
this time!'

'There's something a little odd about our new detective, Charles'

At the end of 1987 there were allegations that Royalty
Protection Squad officers were part of a Masonic conspiracy.

'I love your new hat, darling!'

'*Don't whinge to me about working late, your dinner's in the dustbin*'

'Hope you don't mind, Juan Carlos, these are some people we
met on the plane'

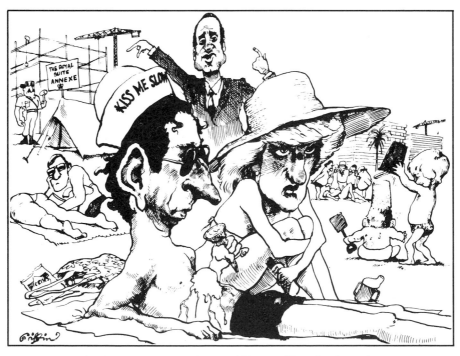

'Well, I think Juan Carlos should have told us they haven't
finished building the Palace'

'Stop showing off, you two!'

'Dad's sketching in Italy, Mummy's out shopping – can I help?'

'*Don't you think Der Highnesses are overdoink it just a
little bit?*'

The Meaning of Life

'Now, my problem is that I have an inherited inability to keep my mouth shut,' said the Prince in a speech at the Building Communities Conference in London in 1986. Over the years he has taken up a number of causes and pronounced on them with a passion and conviction obviously inherited from his father the Duke of Edinburgh. The Duke once claimed, 'I know I'm rude, but it's fun!' – union leader Clive Jenkins described his outspokenness as 'the best argument for republicanism since George III'.

But on a whole range of issues – from 'alternative' medicine and organic farming to solving the problems of youth unemployment and the inner cities – the Prince's concern has attracted wide public following and, on occasions, brought him into conflict with the Establishment. Prince Charles takes as his themes the essence of life, the relationships between mind and body, the individual and the collective, art and the environment, and he likes to challenge conventional wisdom. His *bête noire* is bureaucratic red tape.

Sometimes the Prince's message goes so deep that it can mystify his audience, as when he said to the assembled lumberjacks at the opening of an arts festival in British Columbia: 'Deep in the soul of mankind there is a reflection as on the surface of a mirror, of a mirror-calm lake of the beauty and harmony of the universe. But so often that reflection is obscured and ruffled by unaccountable storms . . . for its seems to me that it is only through the development of an inner peace in the individual, and through the outward manifestation of that reflection, that we can ever hope to attain the kind of peace in this world for which so many yearn.' *Quite!*

While the tabloid Press have sometimes dubbed him 'loony' for his active campaigning for various causes, the overall impression is that the 'caring' Prince is doing the right thing by his future subjects. The results of a National Opinion Poll published early in 1988 showed that 56 per cent of the British population thought he should say more on controversial issues, 57 per cent thought he had too little influence on current affairs, and the view that his opinions are 'peculiar' was rejected by an overwhelming three to one.

Until he becomes King, the Prince has the freedom to express his views and show his compassion as long as it is not in a party political way. Public acclaim for his views on anything from recruiting black guardsmen to banning aerosols in his own home should provide him with considerable encouragement to speak out even more in future.

'Tell Di I'm getting away from it all again for a few weeks!'

*'Charles is in the drawing room with a few of his
Scottish friends!'*

'Oops! Sorry Your Royal Highness!'

'They say that back in the 1980s this used to be the North Sea'

'I talked with a rose that talked with a phlox that talked with the Prince of Wales'

'Charles, have you been talking to the plants again?'

'Have you asked your plant whether it wants a piece of Harry's birthday cake?'

'OK, now that HRH
has made us aware of
the mirror in our souls
reflecting the beauty
and harmony or the
universe – get those
******* trees down!'

`Ever since your swell speech
they've been searching for
inner calm'

'Another royal visit? Don't panic –
Prince Charles often comes down to
have a look'

'Ladies and gentlemen –
pray silence and be upstanding
for the loyal toast . . .'

'*Got any more bright ideas?*'

'*He's obviously finding it hard settling in!*'

RIGHT: *The solicitor's search reveals there are no plans by Prince Charles to set up a scheme for the homeless*

BELOW: '*I know how you feel, Charles, but couldn't we retain just one teensy-weensy little no-go area?*'

'*Charles! Somebody here heard you needed a job*'

Another Charlie

'That? That's one of my gardeners – kept muttering "Prince Charles was right about management".'

'His mother will give him "Up the workers and down with the
bourgeois capitalists" when she gets home'

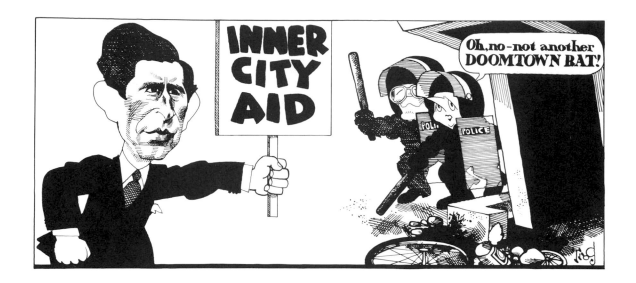

Developers at Six O'Clock

When the cream of the architectural profession and their guests assembled in the courtyard of Hampton Court Palace in 1984, they expected the Prince of Wales to pat them on the back for a job well done and congratulate them on the 150th anniversary of the founding of the Royal Institute of British Architects. But there were a few apprehensive faces in the crowd, because they had already been tipped off about what he was going to say.

'For far too long, it seems to me, some planners and architects have consistently ignored the feelings and wishes of the mass of ordinary people in this country,' he began. In this now infamous attack on modern architecture, planning and development, the Prince went on to condemn the 'monstrous carbuncle' extension proposed for the National Gallery in Trafalgar Square and the 'giant glass stump' proposed by Mies van der Rohe for Mansion House in the City of London. But he also praised the community architecture approach, by which 'ordinary' people are actively involved in the creation and management of their environment.

Apart from inner city regeneration, the Prince has made architecture his main crusade of recent years. He has devoted six major speeches to the subject and no doubt more will follow. Encouraged by the response he has received to his remarks, he has become emboldened: 'I just feel sometimes, not too often, I can throw a rock into a pond and watch the ripples create a certain amount of discussion,' he said tentatively in 1985. By 1987 this sentiment had developed into a wish to 'throw a proverbial royal brick through the inviting plate glass of pompous professional pride'.

On 1 December 1987 the Prince launched his most outspoken assault against what had happened to architecture since the Second World War: 'You have, ladies and gentlemen, to give this much to the Luftwaffe: When it knocked down our buildings, it didn't replace them with anything more offensive than rubble. We did that.' Architects and planners, he went on, 'get whole towns in the family way, pay nothing towards maintenance and call it romance' – the public were left to live in 'the shadows of their achievements'.

Not wishing to be taken for 'an over-zealous convert' to the cause, the Prince nevertheless likes to share his experiences with others. His views on modern architecture have been likened to those of Mrs Mary Whitehouse on Madonna, but when it comes to commissioning architects for his own projects – on the Duchy of Cornwall estate, for example – he practises what he preaches and makes sure they fulfil the wishes of those who live there.

'For heavens's sake, Charles! He's only a child!'

*'I can see a new extension to the National Gallery designed by
Prince Charles – a row of bloody polo stables'*

'It's the redesigned Palumbo Tower!'

LEFT: *'The trouble is, there are a number of inner city sites that are just not available!'*

A FAIRY TALE...

Once upon a time, there lived a King who ruled over a small island. Though he dwelt in a sumptuous palace and was adored by his subjects like a god, the King was troubled...

In ancient times, bands of "magicians" had promised to transform the Kingdom into Utopia by magic, in return for gold.

But the magicians were charlatans, and after they had finished, the country was in a worse state than before.

ARCHITECTURE WILL SOLVE ALL YOUR PROBLEMS!

Now, on his secret coach journeys round the land the King saw a divided realm—soaring towers of the rich on one hand, and no-go troll ghettos on the other.

The King sought advice from all the wise men of the realm, but to no avail. Then, one day, an obscure pedlar called Blackhorse Rod came to the palace...

SIRE, I AM REALLY A WIZARD IN DISGUISE — I HAVE SPECIAL POWERS!

WHAT HAS ONE GOT TO LOSE!?

So Blackhorse Rod became the King's special adviser...

NOW, ROD, WHAT *IS* THIS MAGIC THAT WILL BRING MY SUBJECTS TOGETHER IN HARMONY?

SIRE, IT IS CALLED..

ARCHITECTURE!

Hellman

The offending item in the Prince's soup is an icon of modern architecture, Villa Savoye by Le Corbusier (the garçon).

101

RIGHT: '*I have this re-occurring nightmare that Prince Charles liked one of my buildings*'

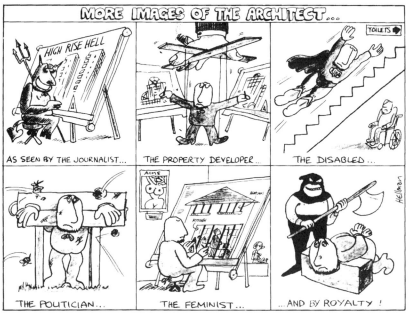

*'Oh! Charles, come and see
what the architects have
put in the garden!'*

*'Actually, Your Highness,
it's against company policy to
apply for a second helping'*

'*Property developers at six o'clock!*'

'*Harry – Prince Charles isn't the only one driven mad by some builders
ignoring the chance to knock down the old and rebuild the new.*'

Royal Rat Pack

Apart from the rare private and unannounced visits, the Royal Family cannot go anywhere without being followed by hordes of Press reporters and photographers. During his first term at Cheam School the Prince featured in no less than sixty-eight stories – a new royal record – and his sense of frivolity soon earned him the nickname the Clown Prince.

Collectively the Press is known as the Royal Rat Pack, but they have been called many others things as well. Prince Philip has likened them to mosquitoes and monkeys and once expressed the wish that a news photographer who fell out of a tree while on a royal assignment broke his 'bloody neck'.

The fact remains that Royalty sells newspapers and the British public has an unquenchable thirst for stories and pictures. On one day in August 1987, twenty-nine photographs appeared in the tabloid Press of the Prince, the Princess, Prince William and Prince Harry. Headline writers can get away with anything: 'Say hello to El Grumpo, the future King of England' whinged the *Star*. Official denials of stories are so rare that the papers take silence as confirmation – members of the Press stated categorically that the Princess of Wales was pregnant at least four times in the first three years of her marriage!

Foreign newspapers share the infatuation. A survey of the French Press for the years 1958 to 1972 showed that during this period the Queen: was pregnant on 92 occasions; had 149 accidents and 9 miscarriages; took the Pill 11 times; was on the verge of abdication 63 times and divorce 73 times; spent 43 unhappy nights; suffered 27 nightmares; received 29 threats to her life; and expelled Lord Snowdon from Court no less than 151 times.

At the time of her engagement, Lady Diana Spencer, then a kindergarten teacher, had her own method of dealing with them: 'I treat the Press as though they were children.' On another occasion she asked the presumably rhetorical question: 'What have the newspapers ever done for me?' The *Sun* replied anyway: 'We can answer Her Loveliness in one word – EVERYTHING!' The time to start worrying, says Prince Charles, would be if the photographers *weren't* interested in the Royal Family's activities.

Still, the Prince did manage to get his own back on one famous occasion, when he was serving in the Royal Navy. His ship was boarded by a party of photographers who were taken to see the duty officer, a young lieutenant. They were told that the Prince did not want to be disturbed by them and, anyway, he was 'pompous' and 'not very bright'. They left empty-handed, not realising that they had been conned – the young lieutenant was none other than the Prince himself!

RIGHT: '*Relax, they're only shooting journalists*'

BELOW: '*There weren't many pheasants around today, but the place was swarming with photographers*'

'I said, "Which way to Balmoral?"'

'I've got this scoop about our loony stories
driving Prince Charles mad'

'You can come down now, Alf – they're engaged'

'I want close-ups of the Princess enjoying
her new freedom from Press
photographers'

'The photographers and reporters are still hanging around, dear.
Only the cartoonists have had the decency to leave
you alone'

'*The usual press rubbish about a royal rift, Your Highness!*'

'*Cut!!!*'

*'I loved how we came over as an ordinary family – you can
change channels now, Smith'*

'One more push, Di, and we'll have 'em!'

'All we said was, "Smile, please."'

'Might one be permitted to know why Your Highness has changed
his mind about doing this scene?'

116

Windsor Tours

Apart from frequent private visits abroad, for example to Italy to study art and architecture and to paint, the Prince has toured the world extensively since his six-month stay at Geelong Grammar School's outback retreat, Timbertop, in Australia in 1966. The country became almost a second home to him.

His first long trip, aged five, was to Malta to meet his parents on their way back from their Coronation Tour of the Commonwealth in 1953. But his most punishing schedule was in 1970, when he was still at university and also learning to fly, when he visited France twice, New Zealand and Australia, Japan, Canada, the United States, Fiji and the Gilbert and Ellis Islands, Bermuda and Barbados, going round the globe three times. 'The whole idea is to meet people and for them to see that I'm a pretty ordinary sort of person and not different from anyone else,' said the Prince. During his 1977 visit to Canberra, it was to meet 'as many people as possible – and this does not exclude eligible young ladies.' Sometimes the going gets quite tough for the Prince, as when he visits the Kalahari Desert with Sir Laurens van der Post, or goes on safari to Kenya, as he did with Princess Anne in 1971: 'It was the best thing I have ever done, or one of the best – the sort of enlightened masochism which I go in for.'

Displays of royal wit are commonplace during what have been dubbed 'Windsor Tours'. Prince Charles quipped, 'Boy, the things I do for England' when he tasted snake meat at a Gurkha training camp in the Far East; finishing a dog-sleigh ride in Canada, he punned, 'That just sleighed me'; and in India, in 1980, he said, 'May the udders of your buffaloes be always full of milk.'

Not wishing to offend their royal guests, hosts are often at pains to point out the quaint procedures of protocol. 'If you find you are to be presented to the Queen, do not rush up to her. She will eventually be brought round to you like a dessert trolley at a good restaurant,' the *Los Angeles Times* helpfully pointed out. Nicknames such as Prince William's Wombat – or Billy the Kid, as the local Australian Press dubbed him – are often born on tours. During a tour of America President Reagan invented the name 'Princess David' for Diana.

Everywhere the Royal Family go there is the smell of fresh paint, which the Prince finds particularly unpleasant. 'It sticks in my nose and makes me feel nauseous,' he says. But there are some benefits when travelling by Windsor Tours: the Princess got to dance with John Travolta at the White House (the photographs were never released); and in 1985 a celebrity event attended by Their Royal Highnesses in Texas helped to raise three million dollars for the Prince's favourite charities.

'So would you *flake out* after a
royal walkabout . . .'

'Nice bit of red carpet . . . expecting
someone?'

'Oh, Jennings, while you're in there, ask HRH Red Crow if I can have my toupee back . . .'

'On your feet, corporal – I'm sure His Royal Highness only gave
you a karate chop for fun'

'Just relaxing, Di, I came over a bit faint!'

*'Must you demonstrate karate while we're having
breakfast, Charles?'*

'Worra lotta b'dong b'dong!'

'The chief says, "What's the chance of getting his daughters
on Page 3!'

'*You will like this, O Prince. We are punishing the camel-rider
who upset you yesterday*'

'You're well guarded but it's best you keep a low profile!'

'OK, you can take the yashmak off now, Diana . . . DIANA?'

*'In the absence of Crown Prince Abdullah, I said, "Who would
you like to sit next to for a chat?"'*

'*Does His Royal Highness do impressions?*'

'*I'm checking we're not related to Mussolini!*'

'*No, no – she's explaining that she would like Wills and Harry to be tall!*'

Austrian Chancellor Sinowatz and Prince Charles – as seen by
Vienna's Die Presse

'*Your Holiness – I fear that there has been a grave mistake . . .*'

'*They said it was too big to go inside!*'

'*Well, I only hope they appreciate the joke, Charles!*'

'*Hope y'don't mind, sports – you were five minutes late, so we
started without you . . .*'

'I thought they could all do with a holiday!'

'Crikey, now she's trying it on the didgeridoo!'

'You sure we need four for our swimming-pool, Di?'

'Quick! Find Willie something else to play with!'

'Sarah Ferguson? . . . No, Your Highness, that's
Davy Crockett'

'*My dance, I think, punk*'

'*I danced with a girl who danced with a man who danced with the Princess of Wales . . .*'

'*I told you she'd get in somehow!*'

'Take it from me, Joan, the age gap won't spoil anything'

The Greatest Show on Earth

These days the life of members of the Royal Family is often compared to a soap opera, a royal version of *Dallas* called *Palace*. But it would be difficult for any team of Hollywood scriptwriters to invent such a family. Notwithstanding their *Spitting Image* counterparts, Prince Charles once pointed out: 'We are a family of human beings, not a set of symbols.'

At the family's head, at least in terms of longevity, is Queen Elizabeth the Queen Mother – 'the most wonderful example of fun, laughter, warmth, infinite security and, above all else, exquisite taste in so many things', according to the Prince. But she can also play the bongo drums and once brought down a rhinoceros with a big game rifle. Then there is the Queen, who once dressed up as a beatnik for a costume party (some years later her daughter-in-law, Princess Diana, and future daughter-in-law, Sarah Ferguson, visited Stringfellow's night-club dressed as women police officers in a much-publicised stunt).

The Queen is rivalled only by her sister, Princess Margaret (known in Palace circles as Charlie's Aunt), in her excellent mimicry, especially of Cockney and American accents. When the family gets together she leads them in their favourite party game of charades, for which they all dress up.

Prince Philip, Duke of Edinburgh, was described (by Bud Flanagan) as 'the working girl's Adam Faith', while Basil Boothroyd, his official biographer, wrote: 'No one has a kinder heart or takes more trouble to conceal it.' When he's in a foul mood, the palace servants call him Annigoni after the stern likeness of the Duke painted by the artist. (The Queen is known as Miss Piggy on similar occasions.)

Through marriage and births, the family grows all the time, of course: Captain Mark Phillips (called Foggy by the Prince, 'because he is thick and wet'), Princess Diana and the Duchess of York, and their respective children, have all joined it recently.

Princess Anne once told royal photographers to 'Naff off!'; she has since blossomed into the Princess Royal with her charity work for Save the Children. Prince Andrew – who grew up from being 'Andy Pandy' to 'Randy Andy' – is 'the one with the Robert Redford looks', as Prince Charles once described him; the Navy helicopter pilot and Falklands War veteran has settled down (well, almost!) with Fergie, or the 'Flying Duchess' as she's sometimes known. And Prince Edward, erstwhile Royal Marine, is making himself really useful as a tea boy in Andrew Lloyd Webber's Really Useful Theatre Company. All the younger children were happy to make royal jesters of themselves in The Grand Knockout Tournament organised by Prince Edward (and raised one million pounds for four charities). Prince Charles sternly declined to appear.

'Il y a toujours un boute-en-train qui met le châpeau des dames
pour amuser la société'
*'There's always some bright spark who'll don a lady's hat to
amuse the crowd'*

'Oh, a red in the top pocket, well done, Di!'

'Keep your wings – I mean your arms – by
your sides, your Royal Highness'

'That's the last time your brother comes here for dinner!'

'She'd never dream of wearing anything as outrageous as this!'

'Shh! We must be close to Princess Michael's apartments now'

'What with Prince Andrew meeting Selina Scott, Anne meeting Wogan and now the Di and
Charles Show, I think someone is feeling a bit left out . . .'

'Don't phone us, we'll phone you – next!'

'Where exactly did your father find this new nanny, Charles?'

'Sorry, darling, it's the best I can do with the staff gone'

'You're new here, aren't you?'

'Can't you have a word with her, Father? – I think she proved her fitness enough with the
lighthouse climb'

'We hear there's someone in the Palace who doesn't back my horses, Charles!'

'Just how much of a flutter did Her Majesty have on Prince Charles on Saturday?'

'*On your toes, everybody – here comes Mr Delfont!*'

♫ 'Singing in the Reign . . .' ♫

*The Princess of Wales gives a fashion display with
"Taffy", the mascot of the Welsh regiment*

'*They've come straight to Ascot from filming* It's a Knockout'

'Never mind the "Isn't-that-Lady-Di-with-him" – run for it'

'Hats off and stand to attention everybody – it's Di and Fergie!'

'I thought this idea might interest you, Mark!'

'There was a big changing of the guard yesterday, Sir . . .'

'The photographers have gone, you can come in now, Andy'

'Once you start sponsorship it never ends!'

Hard times

'Right! You see that, you 'orrible lot? Miss Fergie's got the right idea'

One's Destiny

Dining at Chequers with the Prime Minister, Mr. James Callaghan, and some of his Cabinet in 1977, Prince Charles declared that he had 'a rotten, boring job'. An unidentified Labour minister tweaked him on the cheek and said: 'Well, you shouldn't have taken the job then, should you?' As he enters his forty-first year, the Prince is aware that his position as Prince of Wales – without a predetermined role and with no constitutional authority – could quite possibly last a further twenty years or more.

But, as the Prince once admitted, the source of some frustration for him is also a blessing in disguise: 'There isn't any power. But there can be influence. The influence is in direct proportion to the respect people have for you.' He decided to tackle his role in three ways: 'to show concern for people, to display an interest in them as individuals, and to encourage them in a whole host of ways'.

In the recent past this has made him both a 'jack-of-all-trades', and someone who is occasionally prepared to stick his neck out on important and controversial issues. Previous bearers of his title have, for the most part, frittered their lives away or spent their time satisfying over-active libidos.

One day King Charles III will inherit all the cares of State, but have far less influence than he enjoys now. He will also inherit one of the largest private fortunes in the world, estimated at some £4,500 million. He has, of course, already performed his most important function – the continuation of his line – by producing 'an heir and a spare'. What occupies his time and energy until he succeeds to the throne is a source of constant anxiety; it is also said to be causing his advisers and government some anxiety . . . He often talks about being 'imprisoned' or 'confined' by his job. He 'lacks confidence', say his friends.

Sometimes, when the Prince receives as good as he gives from those who are subjected to his verbal muggings on important issues, he threatens to give up – and many politicians no doubt hope he might. Interviewed on BBC Radio 4 after his 'Luftwaffe' speech at the end of 1987, he said: 'Clearly it would be easier to lead a quiet life. I don't need to do all this, you know. I mean, nobody's ordering me to go and do it. There's no set royal function. It's just that I feel strongly for better or worse about a lot of these things. I mean, if you go around the country in my position . . . I've learned a lot, I've looked a lot, I can't just sit there and do nothing about it. But if they'd rather I did nothing about it, I'll go off somewhere else.'

With all the skill of a seasoned performer the Prince left his audience clamouring for more.

The Lifer

'Is it really true that one day all this will be mine?'

'*Charles, I've told you before – "Sospan fach" is*
not *the National Anthem*'

'*We are honoured by this surprise visit, Your Majesty!*'

'To the great surprise of her subjects, on the occasion of her
100th birthday, Queen Elizabeth II abdicates the throne of
England in favour of her young son, Prince Charles aged 78.'

Index: Copyrights

Unknown: 16 TOP LHS **Sally Artz:** 40 TOP **Building:** 93 TOP **Building Design:** 101 **Cartoon-Caricature-Contor:** 17, 75 TOP, 159 **Calman:** 9, 36 TOP, 96 LHS, 105 TOP **Chic:** 146 BOTTOM **Daily Express:** 21, 24 BOTTOM, 25 BOTTOM, 28, 30 TOP, 34 TOP LHS, 34 BOTTOM, 37 BOTTOM, 41 BOTTOM, 43, 45 BOTTOM, 47 TOP, 54, 59 BOTTOM, 60, 64 TOP LHS, 64 TOP RHS, 71 TOP, 74 TOP, 76 TOP, 76 BOTTOM, 84 BOTTOM, 89 BOTTOM, 90 BOTTOM, 97 BOTTOM, 105 BOTTOM, 114 BOTTOM, 115 BOTTOM, 120, 125 TOP, 131 BOTTOM, 140 BOTTOM, 142 TOP, 144 TOP, 149 **Daily Herald:** 18 **Daily Mail:** Front cover, Back cover, 20 LHS, 24 TOP, 25 TOP, 26 TOP RHS, 26 BOTTOM, 30 BOTTOM, 42 BOTTOM, 47 BOTTOM, 63 BOTTOM, 65 TOP, 65 BOTTOM, 66 BOTTOM, 67 BOTTOM, 77, 82, 84 TOP, 85 TOP, 85 BOTTOM, 87 RHS, 88 BOTTOM, 91, 92 TOP, 94 RHS, 96 RHS, 97 TOP, 99 TOP LHS, 108 BOTTOM, 112 BOTTOM, 119, 125 BOTTOM, 129, 130 BOTTOM, 141, 144 BOTTOM, 145 BOTTOM, 151 **Daily Mirror:** 139 TOP RHS **Daily Telegraph:** 51 TOP, 51 BOTTOM, 55 TOP LHS, 59 TOP LHS, 83 TOP LHS, 83 TOP RHS, 94 LHS, 128, 135 TOP, 146 TOP, 158 **Barry Fantoni:** 13 **The Guardian:** 27 **Louis Hellman:** 92 BOTTOM, 99 BOTTOM, 100, 102 BOTTOM, 106 **Jon:** 44 RHS, 157 TOP LHS **Langdon:** 41 TOP LHS, 118 TOP **London Daily News:** 111 RHS TOP **London Express News & Feature Services:** 20 RHS **Mac:** 35 LHS **Marc:** Front cover **Paul-Henri Moisan:** 138 **Neblespalter:** 56 LHS **The Observer:** Back Cover, 156 BOTTOM, 157 BOTTOM **Pelham Books:** 16 BOTTOM **Private Eye:** 10, 55 BOTTOM, 59 TOP RHS, 89 TOP **Punch:** 2, 8, 16 TOP RHS, 22/23, 40 BOTTOM RHS, 48, 53, 53 BOTTOM, 58 RHS, 86, 110, 111 LHS, 111 RHS BOTTOM, 126 TOP LHS, 127, 148 TOP, 156 TOP RHS **Rausch:** 160 **Scarfe:** 6, 11 **The Standard:** 36 BOTTOM, 98, 103 TOP, 104, 114 TOP **The Sun:** 33 BOTTOM LHS, 33 BOTTOM RHS, 34 TOP RHS, 35 RHS TOP, 35 RHS BOTTOM, 37 TOP, 38 RHS, 41 TOP RHS, 42 TOP, 44 LHS TOP, 44 LHS BOTTOM, 45 TOP, 46 TOP, 46 BOTTOM LHS, 46 BOTTOM RHS, 52 TOP, 52 BOTTOM, 55 TOP RHS, 56 RHS TOP, 56 RHS BOTTOM, 57 TOP, 57 BOTTOM LHS, 57 BOTTOM RHS, 58 LHS, 62 LHS TOP, 62 LHS BOTTOM, 63 TOP LHS, 63 TOP RHS, 66 RHS, 67 TOP LHS, 69 TOP, 69 BOTTOM, 71 BOTTOM, 72 BOTTOM, 75 BOTTOM, 80 TOP, 80 BOTTOM, 87 LHS TOP, 87 LHS BOTTOM, 90 TOP, 112 TOP, 113, 115 TOP, 116 TOP, 118 BOTTOM, 121 TOP, 122 TOP, 122 BOTTOM, 124 TOP, 124 BOTTOM, 126 TOP RHS, 126 BOTTOM, 130 TOP LHS, 130 TOP RHS, 131 TOP, 132 TOP LHS, 132 TOP RHS, 132 BOTTOM, 135 BOTTOM, 139 TOP LHS, 140 TOP, 145 TOP, 147, 150 TOP, 152 TOP LHS, 152 TOP RHS, 152 BOTTOM, 153 TOP, 153 BOTTOM, 157 TOP RHS **Syndication International:** 14, 26 TOP LHS, 29 TOP, 29 BOTTOM, 32 TOP, 32 BOTTOM, 33 TOP, 38 LHS, 40 BOTTOM LHS, 50, 62 RHS, 64 BOTTOM, 68 TOP, 68 BOTTOM, 70, 72 TOP, 73, 74 BOTTOM, 78, 81 TOP, 81 BOTTOM, 83 BOTTOM, 103 BOTTOM, 108 TOP, 109, 116 BOTTOM, 121 BOTTOM, 123, 133, 134, 136, 139 BOTTOM, 142 BOTTOM, 143, 148 BOTTOM, 150 BOTTOM, 154 **The Times:** 88 TOP RHS, 102 TOP RHS **Trog:** 1, 93 BOTTOM **Waite:** 156 TOP LHS

The publishers have taken all possible care to trace and acknowledge the sources of the illustrations. If any errors have accidentally occurred, we shall be happy to correct them in future editions, provided that we receive notification.

Index: Cartoonists/Artists

Anon: 93 TOP, 128 **Sally Artz:** 40 TOP **Rex Audley:** 55 TOP LHS **Fritz Behrendt:** 16 TOP RHS **Josef Blaumeiser:** 17 **Caldwell:** 34 TOP LHS, 37 BOTTOM, 64 TOP LHS, 64 TOP RHS, 71 TOP, 74 TOP, 76 TOP, 76 BOTTOM, 84 BOTTOM, 89 BOTTOM, 114 BOTTOM, 115 BOTTOM, 125 TOP, 140 BOTTOM, 142 TOP, 144 TOP **Mel Calman:** 9, 36 TOP, 96 LHS, 105 TOP **Chic:** 146 BOTTOM **Cookson:** 69 TOP, 87 LHS BOTTOM, 130 TOP RHS **Dickinson:** 111 LHS, 111 RHS BOTTOM **Dredge:** 59 TOP RHS **Emmwood:** 24 TOP, 25 TOP, 26 TOP RHS, 26 BOTTOM **Barry Fantoni:** 13, 88 TOP RHS, 102 TOP RHS **Evan Ferguson:** 101 **Franklin:** 14, 26 TOP LHS, 29 TOP, 29 BOTTOM, 33 BOTTOM LHS, 34 TOP RHS, 35 RHS TOP, 35 RHS BOTTOM, 37 TOP, 38 RHS, 41 TOP RHS, 42 TOP, 44 LHS TOP, 44 LHS BOTTOM, 46 BOTTOM LHS, 46 BOTTOM RHS, 52 TOP, 52 BOTTOM, 55 TOP RHS, 56 RHS TOP, 56 RHS BOTTOM, 57 TOP, 57 BOTTOM LHS, 57 BOTTOM RHS, 58 LHS, 62 LHS TOP, 62 LHS BOTTOM, 66 TOP RHS, 69 BOTTOM, 71 BOTTOM, 72 BOTTOM, 75 BOTTOM, 80 TOP, 81 BOTTOM, 87 LHS TOP, 90 TOP, 112 TOP, 113, 115 TOP, 116 TOP, 118 BOTTOM, 121 TOP, 121 BOTTOM, 122 TOP, 124 TOP, 124 BOTTOM, 126 TOP RHS, 130 TOP LHS, 131 TOP, 132 TOP RHS, 132 BOTTOM, 135 BOTTOM, 145 TOP, 147, 152 TOP LHS, 152 TOP RHS, 153 TOP, 153 BOTTOM, 157 TOP RHS **Fritz:** 16 TOP LHS **Gale:** 83 TOP RHS **Garland:** 51 BOTTOM **Gibbard:** 27 **Giles:** 21, 24 BOTTOM, 25 BOTTOM, 28, 30 TOP, 34 BOTTOM, 41 BOTTOM, 43, 45 BOTTOM, 47 TOP, 54, 59 BOTTOM, 60, 90 BOTTOM, 97 BOTTOM, 105 BOTTOM, 120, 131 BOTTOM, 149 **Griffin:** 32 BOTTOM, 64 BOTTOM, 68 TOP, 68 BOTTOM, 70, 72 TOP, 73, 74 BOTTOM, 81 TOP, 83 BOTTOM, 103 BOTTOM, 116 BOTTOM, 123, 133, 134, 136, 139 TOP RHS, 139 BOTTOM, 142 BOTTOM, 143, 148 BOTTOM, 154 **Waltner Hanel:** 75 TOP **Harpur:** 48 **Louis Hellman:** 92 BOTTOM, 99 BOTTOM, 100, 102 BOTTOM, 106 **Tony Holland:** 51 TOP, 59 TOP LHS **Illingworth:** 22/23 **Jak:** 36 BOTTOM, 98, 103 TOP, 114 TOP **Johnston:** 104, 132 TOP LHS **Jon:** 44 RHS, 157 TOP LHS **JUSP:** 56 LHS **Langdon:** 41 TOP LHS, 118 TOP **Joe Lee:** 20 RHS **Mac:** Back cover, 35 LHS, 42 BOTTOM, 47 BOTTOM, 63 BOTTOM, 65 TOP, 65 BOTTOM, 66 BOTTOM, 67 BOTTOM, 77, 82, 84 TOP, 85 TOP, 85 BOTTOM, 88 BOTTOM, 91, 97 TOP, 108, 112 BOTTOM, 119, 125 BOTTOM, 129, 130 BOTTOM, 141, 144 BOTTOM, 145 BOTTOM, 151 **Mahood:** 53 BOTTOM, 58 RHS, 87 RHS, 96 RHS, 99 TOP LHS, 126 TOP LHS, 148 TOP **Marc:** FRONT COVER, 94 LHS, 146 TOP **C L Mays:** 8 **Stan McMurtry:** 86 **Moi San:** 138 **NEB:** 20 LHS **Newman:** 89 TOP, 111 RHS TOP **Rausch:** 160 **Rigby:** 45 TOP, 46 TOP **Roberts:** 78 **William Rushton:** 10, 16 BOTTOM, 55 BOTTOM **Gerald Scarfe:** 6, 11 **Oliver Schopf:** 159 **E H Shepard:** 2 **Ben Snails:** 83 TOP, 135 TOP **John Springs:** 158 **Ken Taylor:** 33 TOP, 127 **Trog:** Front cover, Back cover, 1, 30 BOTTOM, 40 BOTTOM LHS, 92 TOP, 93 BOTTOM, 94 RHS, 110, 156 RHS, 156 BOTTOM, 157 BOTTOM **B Von Keusch:** 16 TOP RHS **Waite:** 32 TOP, 38 LHS, 40 BOTTOM LHS, 50, 62 RHS, 108 TOP, 109, 150 BOTTOM, 156 TOP LHS **Gilbert Wilkinson:** 18 **Zoke:** 33 BOTTOM RHS, 63 TOP LHS, 63 TOP RHS, 67 TOP LHS, 80 BOTTOM, 122 TOP, 126 BOTTOM, 139 TOP LHS, 140 TOP, 150 TOP, 152 BOTTOM